Jacky Warwicker is a retired drama teacher living in North East England.

Through writing, she has discovered a new way of communicating with an audience. Believing that art is an integral part of life, she wrote *Journey's Bend* as a creative outlet.

In addition to exploring places of cultural interest, Jacky enjoys going to the theatre, reading and walking.

For my family, a constant source of joy.

Jacky Warwicker

Journey's Bend

Austin Macauley Publishers™

LONDON • CAMBRIDGE • NEW YORK • SHARJAH

A CIP catalogue record for this title is available from the British Library.

ISBN 9781398404939 (Paperback)
ISBN 9781398404946 (ePub e-book)

www.austinmacauley.com

First Published 2023
Austin Macauley Publishers Ltd®
1 Canada Square
Canary Wharf
London
E14 5AA

Special thanks to Mick for his unwavering support and encouragement.

Table of Contents

The Last Stretch

Meg's flaming orange hair glowed like a firework in the dark corner of the room. 'A goat being imprisoned for armed robbery in Nigeria is not small stuff,' she said. 'How would you like to go to jail for something you haven't done?'

'There are far bigger things to worry about, like rescuing Gran from incarceration,' Angie replied.

'I hope you're not planning to bust her out of the care home.'

'Now there's an idea,' Angie said with a gleam in her eye.

'Just give Gran some time, she's adjusting to losing Grandad that's all.'

'She's in the wrong place Meg, she'll never thrive in there.'

'Gran's irrepressible, she'll spring back to life.'

'What if she doesn't?' Angie asked. 'Gran's the heart and soul of the family, I'm not risking her happiness.'

Driving to Gran's care home, Angie chortled at the *Adventure Before Dementia* sticker on the camper van rattling past her.

Shame Gran sits lifeless in that stuffy, drab room watching wall-to-wall tele, she thought ruefully. Angie remembered the old Elsie, quick as a whippet, trotting to the pub for a reviving bottle of stout in rummage sale glad rags and pinky pearl earrings.

'Don't give in Gran,' she called out, 'grab some fun in your twilight years.'

Angie blocked out the sound of her ringing phone to concentrate on the tricky parallel parking. A smug looking bloke on the pavement smirked as he watched her struggle with the manoever. After several attempts, she backed into the tight space and returned the call. 'Hi, Mum. Is everything alright?' she asked swiftly.

'It's your gran, she's absconded from the care home with a shopping trolley full of clothes,' her mother said. Angie resisted the temptation to whoop in delight at Gran's indomitable spirit of rebellion.

'Why would she just take off like that?' her mother snapped. 'I thought she'd settled in.' Angie winced at her folly. Since the promotion, she'd been consumed by her job to the detriment of Gran's welfare.

'I know the staff are fantastic Mum but the care home doesn't suit her,' Angie said candidly. 'I'll help find Gran but I'm not taking her back there.'

Skilfully using her walking frame, Hilda came towards Angie like a well-coordinated stick insect.

'I know where Elsie is,' she said voluntarily, pleased to be a bearer of good news. 'She's gone to North Shields to buy the Reliant Robin she saw on eBay.'

Angie buzzed with pride; Gran had used the internet to track down an epochal vehicle from her courtship days. With adroit fingers, she located the seller of the risible three-wheeled car on her mobile. Angie thought of Elsie in the confines of her room, packing her shopping trolley full of clothes, ready for the big escape. '*I want to break free,*' she sang, thrilled by Gran's rousing adventure.

Driving along the coast road, Angie caught sight of a lone surfer cruising like a sleek seal through the choppy waves. To the sound of a malfunctioning Sat Nav, she stopped the car adjacent to the long stretch of golden sands aligning the bay. Harmonious white clouds burst from their horizontal bases to canopy the sky. In a fleeting moment of rapture, she saw her tiny hand in Gran's as they raced breathless to the sea. *Happy days will come again,* Angie told herself as she searched for a trusty map.

With mounting excitement, she plotted her route to the Meadow Well, famous for riots and strong, vigilant women. By now, Gran would be haggling over the price of her purchase, bent on getting a good deal as in her glory days, when she trounced hard-nosed marketeers. 'Good old Elsie,' Angie cheered, proud of her feisty roots.

The shopping trolley perched on the passenger seat looked like a sentinel dog wanting a ride. Gran was circling the vehicle, checking the tyres and bodywork before parting with her meagre nest egg. By the time Angie crossed the busy road, she'd bought the red Reliant Robin, a touching insignia of her prime. Away from the care home, Gran hugged her with renewed vigour, 'Ya mam rang to say you'd be coming, do you like my new car?'

'What a beauty,' Angie said, surveying the fragile vehicle with sensible trepidation.

'Just like ya grandad drove back in the day, when we first met.'

'What are you going to do with it, Gran?'

'Drive it, of course. I'm going to the Lake District to speak to ya grandad, I can't hear a word he's saying in the care home. It's where we went on our first holiday together; we'll be able to have a good chat on our special path above Rydal Water.'

'I've been so busy rushing abroad every holiday, I haven't been to The Lakes in years.'

Gran took her arm, 'Come with me pet, it will do you the world of good slowing down. I'm borrowing ya uncle Mike's whippet for the trip, better than any medication watching her scamper up the hills.'

'A brindle whippet, just like Joey,' Angie said, succumbing to the rolling flow of events.

Not in the same league as a durable camper van, the three-wheeled car swayed erratically in the gusty winds mauling Ambleside. Gran, wobbling like a child on a roller coaster, gripped the steering wheel tightly with her bony hands. The refined face of the whippet nuzzling between the front seats eased Angie's rumbling anxiety.

Relieved at the sight of the time-warped hotel, they made light of Gran scraping the car against the low stone wall. In the crisp October air, Angie recognised the ruffled bells of the clematis trailing the entrance. Recalling the newspaper story, she looked for the infamous cottage nestled in the grounds.

'A member of staff harbouring a friend led to Sonia's death,' Gran said, following her gaze. Thoughts of the hotelier, murdered in her abode by a hidden resident, hovered around Angie like a menacing sceptre. A silver-grey cat stirring beneath the weathered sundial, dispelled her gloom.

'As you know bad things happen and life moves on,' Gran remarked.

Neither of them repositioned the sprawling whippet at the bottom of the bed making it difficult for them to stretch their legs.

'To Grandad,' Angie said, clinking Gran's stout with her wine glass. 'May his spirit bound up the hills forever.' They smiled widely as a respectful hush settled over them.

'What do you want to talk to Grandad about?' Angie asked, breaking the silence.

'It's difficult without him,' Gran answered, savouring the familiar taste of creamy stout. 'I want to know how I can make the journey alone.'

'You're not alone, Gran,' Angie consoled, 'you've got a loving family. Don't go back to the care home, grab yourself some adventure.'

'I feel washed up in a foreign land, unable to speak the language,' Gran said, stroking the whippet. Angie bridled at the truth of Gran's words. When Justine died, grief had washed away all perimeters, leaving her in alien territory. She obliterated images of her girlfriend's skeletal corpse in the hospital bed and saw instead, soft curls framing her radiant face.

'I imagined Justine flying this earth with our future tucked under her wings but she's never left my side,' Angie confided. Gran rested her head on the oversized pillow, listening attentively to her intimate story. 'The other day in class, a girl threw a high heeled shoe at the back of my head making it bleed. I pleaded for Justine's help and a transforming calmness settled in the room, filling me with courage.'

'I don't know how you work with those troubled girls,' Gran said, 'but I'm proud that you do. We'll have a lovely walk tomorrow pet; me, you and the dog.'

The wind had abated, leaving autumn to blaze in all her glory when they took the ascending path out of Ambleside. The agile whippet bounded ahead, snuffling in the tawny bracken before charging up the hill with exhilarating speed. Dazzling golden leaves spread like nature's treasure over the rocky stones embedded in the ground.

'To think on my first visit to The Lakes I wore fashionable shoes, trying to look glamorous,' Gran said with a chuckle. 'Ya grandad bought me my first pair of walking boots so I could keep abreast with his practised strides.' Angie pictured them walking and talking as they'd done all their married lives, in the changing seasons of their journey together.

They reached the outskirts of Rydal Mount where Wordsworth resided with his family; "The loveliest spot that man hath ever found," he wrote, eulogising the splendour of the place. Angie knew about the hundreds of daffodils the poet had planted in Dora's Field, in memory of his beloved daughter. *A host of golden flowers, fluttering and dancing in death's breeze*, she thought. 'Do you want to stop for coffee?' Angie asked Gran, hoping to visit the tranquil tearoom where Dora took her lessons.

'If you don't mind, I want to reach Loughrigg Terrace before the light begins to fade,' she answered. With the whippet trotting faithfully by their side, they fell into companionable silence, awed by the natural beauty of resplendent Rydal.

Angie looked up from retying her bootlaces; Gran was perched on the warped bench overlooking Grasmere with Grandad's black and white scarf wrapped around her neck. A rainbow arched over majestic Silver How like a shimmering tiara crowning the land. Angie hovered in the background, whilst Gran searched the intricate map of life for a way forward. The whippet ran maniacally between the two of them deciding where to settle. By the time they huddled together on the bench, Gran had chosen a fresh untrodden path for the last stretch of her journey.

'You're never too old to root for the Toon, paddle in a stream or laugh aloud with the bairns,' she said, sounding like Grandad. 'I'm going to live each day as if it's my last. So long, care home. Hello, beautiful life.'

Angie unravelled the football scarf from Gran's neck and held it above their heads. 'Don't stop me now,' she sang as the whippet head-butted the swaying banner.

Recalled Home

The brightly inscribed box looked like a Christmas present waiting to be stacked under the tree. Martin carried it into the garden, half expecting to see the dead cat preening herself on the stone wall. Ella watched earnestly as he placed the package in the freshly dug grave.

'Holly's days have run out, Daddy,' she said, motionless until an afterthought made her start. 'I hope pussy doesn't steal the sausages in heaven,' she added, recalling the cat's artful theft at the barbecue. Consoled by the innocence of her remark, Martin shovelled rich brown soil into the exposed ground, shrouding the box.

In the restful house, Ella sprawled on the floor drawing a vivid picture of her lost pet. Taking care to use all the paper as her mammy taught her, she captured the intricate patterns of Holly's tortoiseshell fur. Martin was in the kitchen making sandwiches when an old lady in a compact brown beret scurried up the path. 'This is it,' she called breezily to her trailing sister, 'this is the house where we were born.' Disorientated by the incongruity of their appearance, Martin started swilling the lettuce until their joyful aplomb secured his full attention.

Like two tabbies intent on making themselves comfortable, the sisters settled serenely on the sofa. Ella smiled at them shyly as she sauntered into the kitchen cloaked in the cat's hairy blanket. They suited their quaint, old fashioned names Martin thought, Edith and Agnes, the "blessed" and the "pure" in etymological terms. He lifted his recent eBay acquisition from the mantelpiece, a tarnished postcard of Alnmouth beach fringed with sentinel villas. 'Did a bracing walk to Boulmer today but haven't yet braved the sea,' Martin read in his lilting Geordie accent.

'I'll be home for lunch on Sunday when I'll give you all my news. Love, Daisy.' The sisters gawped in delight at the unexpected souvenir of their mam's sojourn on the Northumberland Coast.

'How marvellous,' they chirped in perfect unison, relishing the coincidence of their timely visit.

'Mam met Dad on that holiday, he was a baker and lavished her cakes with extra cream, melting her heart,' Agnes enthused. 'We moved to Alnmouth when Edie was two years old, she can't remember the pit wheel turning or Tappy Jack lighting the lamps. It was spellbinding when he reached up with his long pole and magicked golden stars on a pitch-black night.'

Martin struggled to equate the beneficent lamplighter with the man posthumously belittled in pubs for his eccentricity. He didn't divulge the tragic circumstances of Jack's last days when he used the floorboards to kindle his fire, safekeeping a wooden platform for his armchair.

'It all looks and sounds so different now,' Agnes observed. 'No smoking chimney stacks besmirching the clear blue sky. No matchstick men with cold tea tied to their belts trudging to and from the pits.' Martin could visualise the stout-hearted miners of the North East making their way to back-breaking work beneath the earth. 'Granda bathed in a zinc bath on a peg rug in this very room. In front of a crackling fire, he washed his panda eyes before scrubbing his coal-stained body.' *What's to show of this industrial heritage,* Martin wondered, *a bright-red pit wheel like a relic from a funfair, standing unmarked on tufty grass.*

Ella, generations removed from the child trappers who crouched in the pit's blackness, strolled into the sunny room.

'Daddy, when can I have a new kitten?' she asked, glancing over at the unified sisters with a modicum of interest.

'We're sorry to hear about your cat, my dear,' Edith consoled.

'Holly was old, it was her time to go,' Ella explained matter-of-factly to the elderly lady.

'We've taken in a stray cat who's about to have kittens,' Agnes disclosed before catching Martin's wary eye.

'Oh, Daddy, can I have one?' she pleaded, wrapping her arms around his neck to procure the right answer.

'We'll talk to Mammy about it when she gets home,' Martin promised, wanting his wife's blessing for the arrival of a new family member.

'Go outside and play, it's such a glorious day,' he coaxed, recalling the child trappers ensnared in the dark clutches of the pit.

The sisters shuffled their tiny feet before leaning forward on the sofa to make their announcement. 'We want to buy the house,' they said with curious confidence.

'We need to leave Alnmouth, Edith's become afraid of the waves, she thinks they're going to swamp the villa and carry us out to sea,' Agnes confided. Martin felt caught in the lap of a dream, ferrying him beyond reason. With trusting expectancy, they waited silently for him to speak.

'But it isn't for sale,' he said tenderly as if explaining something complex to Ella.

'The house is calling us, it wants us to move back in and end our days here,' Agnes said wittingly.

'If ever we want to sell, you will be the first to know,' he soothed, thinking of his transience in the family home.

In childlike reverie, Edith reached into her bag, 'Ella can play with my corn dolly until we move in,' she said, handing him the figurine. Agnes scribbled their address and telephone number on the back of a faded shop receipt.

'Let me know when we can buy the house,' she instructed cheerily, 'and ring me if you want a kitten.' Watching Agnes pull on the onion-tight beret, Martin contemplated the layers of her personality. He found it unfathomable, lucid memory awash with strange imaginings.

On her return from work, Kate picked up the corn dolly, 'My grandma used to make these,' she said affectionately.

'She had a canny way of twisting the long stalks into figurines with round heads and flowing skirts. Traditionally, they get buried in the earth to secure a strong harvest, I wonder why Edith wanted to leave it in the house?'

'They think they're going to end their days here,' Martin explained, raising his eyebrows to convey the bewildering eccentricity of the sisters.

'I'm sorry I was late home, I got away on time but there was a horrendous traffic jam on the A1, was Ella sad about Holly?'

'Surprisingly placid, she said, "her days have run out, Daddy" with total acceptance. I keep expecting to see Holly squeeze through the cat flap and walk between my legs. Ella's excited about getting a new kitten, I said I'd talk to you about it.'

'Let's leave it for a while, I don't want a new pet just yet. Can't believe I missed her bedtime again but this job feels like a lifeline after the redundancy.'

'Perhaps we should move closer to Durham now I'm working from home,' he suggested, wanting to lighten her load.

'No, I love this house and the village. A move would be too disruptive, I'm not ready to face another major change. Plus, Ella's happy at nursery,' Kate said, picking up the colourful drawing of Holly. In eerie silence, they peered through the window at their cat's tiny grave beneath the yellow chains of the laburnum tree.

The mug cocooned in newspaper resembled an ice cream before Kate stripped it to read the eye-catching story. Banksy's shredded painting of a girl letting go of a heart-shaped red balloon sold at auction for £1,042,000. Feeling the pressure of making a living in a talent-saturated world, she recoiled at the value of the art intervention.

'Oh, Martin, it breaks my heart to leave our first family home but I can't turn down the offer of a permanent full-time job. Those months of unemployment made me feel like I was on a festering scrap heap, rotting away.'

'We won't be leaving our happiness here, Kate, we're moving to a new exciting phase of our lives in beautiful

County Durham. Besides, it's written in the stars, the sisters are returning to end their days where it all began.'

'*To arrive where we started. And know the place for the first time,*' [1]she said, galvanising the energy for their own continuing journey. As Kate wrapped the crockery with renewed vigour, Martin placed the corn dolly on the mantelpiece next to the postcard. Scanning the message on the back, he pictured Daisy in the darkness of a lamp-studded night, calling her bairns home to the safety of the house.

---

[1] T.S. Eliot, from *Little Gidding, Four Quartets* (Gardners Books; Main edition, April 30, 2001) Originally published 1943.

Purple Ribbon

Jeannie watched the rehearsal intently, knowing she had chosen to stage the play in remembrance of Adam. She heard his voice intoning the dialogue with arresting pathos:

'Into my heart an air that kills
From yon far country blows;
What are those blue remembered hills?
What spires, what farms are those?'[2]

Seeing adult actors play ebullient children, transported her back to the Forest of Dean, a place of unforgettable torment for Adam. Jeannie recalled the two of them standing as child evacuees on the precipice of change, waiting to be chosen by eyeballing strangers. As potent memories of her own wartime experience surged over the present, she echoed the narrator's words:

---

[2] Poem XL from *A Shropshire Land* by A.E. Houseman, originally published in 1896. Also featured in *Blue Remembered Hills* by Dennis Potter, originally broadcast on 30 January 1979.

'That is the land of lost content,
I see it shining plain,
The happy highways where I went,
And cannot come again.'[3]

The female artist arrived late, parked her pram bursting with canvasses at the back of the hall and joined the villagers perusing the newcomers. Like a spry scarecrow in an oversized farmer's coat, she pointed to my purple ribbon, rejoicing that it was her favourite colour. Visualising my mother carefully tying the adornment in my hair, I didn't see Adam make his ill-fated exit.

Oblivious to his plight, I settled quickly into my new home at the edge of the forest. I didn't mind the toilet being half-way up the garden because my warm-hearted host turned everything into an adventure. Sweeping the parlour, Rita pretended to be a cranky witch shooing an errant cat from under her feet. Feeding the hens, she greeted them by name before adding melodious trills to their raucous clucking. Afterwards, sitting by the kitchen stove, we invented stories about the chatty birds whilst dunking soldiers into runny eggs.

Thanks to Rita's ingenuity and kindness, I was a thriving evacuee, safe from the perils of the war.

Crunching through multi-coloured autumn leaves, I thought about Adam's disclosure in the school yard. After chopping wood, ravenously hungry, he was sent to the scullery to eat one slice of bread and lard for his evening meal. Solemnly, Adam told me he was shunned by the family and got locked

---

[3] ibid

in his bedroom when they went out. What hurt him most, he said, was that his brutish host kept all the money and parcels sent by his mam. Noticing Adam wince in pain, I enveloped him in my scarf to stave off his loneliness.

'Write home,' I urged, already believing in the power of the pen.

'I do,' he sighed, 'but Mr Fraser checks my letters and makes me change the bits he doesn't like.'

Adam's stark words ringing in my ears, I ran as fast as I could to tell Rita about his predicament.

Indignant on his behalf, she sprang immediately into action. 'Don't take your coat off Jeannie, we're going to rescue Adam from that heinous bully. He's not staying another night in that Godforsaken place.'

Uncharacteristically agitated, Rita charged to the Fraser place with surefooted alacrity to accomplish her mission.

I imagined her kicking down Adam's bedroom door like a superhero and was relieved to see his stooping figure raking the fallen leaves. He started like a frightened rabbit at the sound of our gravelly footsteps.

'We've come to rescue you, Adam,' I called out wanting to assuage his fear.

When Rita finished outlining her escape plan, he glanced nervously towards the house before bolting down the hill to the spinney. By the time his thuggish host appeared in the doorway, Adam was safely harboured in the tranquillity of the coppice.

Despite the comfort of Rita's cottage, in his dreams, he was locked in a collapsing bedroom as Mr Fraser's malevolent shadow darted around him. Adam didn't tell me about the bedwetting but I observed his morning ritual of

26

pounding the dolly-peg in a large tub to clean his soiled sheet. In the yard, Rita helped him rotate the sturdy mangle which squeezed the bedding so tight it emerged like a slice of ice.

In the spring, Adam made a special friend, a German prisoner of war working on a nearby farm. Rita had been commissioned to do a series of paintings depicting wartime Britain and the athletic, Aryan pilot working in the fields was one of her subjects. Whilst Rita packed away her paints, he affectionately tousled Adam's hair, trying hard to engage him in conversation. Undeterred by his monosyllabic responses, the benevolent German threw a football at Adam's feet, kickstarting their friendship.

When the amicable POWs formed their own football team, Adam was the chosen mascot who accompanied them onto the pitch. Wearing the black and red bobble hat knitted by his mam, he was the lucky talisman who heralded the game.

At the blow of the whistle, the fast, zigzagging, ball united the players in steely concentration, effacing all memory of war.

Strong smelling lavender from the well-tended garden, adjacent to the prisoner huts, reminded Stefan of home.

'I have a son the same age as you, Adam,' he said proudly before imparting his sorrow. 'I long to hear how my family are doing in Dresden but there is no news. War feels like a dark endless tunnel from which there is no escape. I do not know when I will be released to see my beautiful boy again.'

We fell into harmonising silence, trying to lighten Stefan's pain.

On her visits, Mam always wore a pretty frock and her best pearl earrings in honour of the occasion. Breathing in her city sophistication, I longed to be back in exhilarant urban streets pulsating with life. Cocooned in Gloucestershire, I was oblivious to the scale of ruination and loss wreaked by intensive enemy bombing. Hearing Mam whisper to Rita that they were trying to finish off Bristol, I just thought she meant completing building work on the harbourside. Thinking I'd gone into the garden instead of lingering behind the door, Mam's voice became loaded with emotion.

'The medieval city was a raging inferno,' she mourned, 'the red sky of Bristol could be seen for miles around.' I heard Rita gasp.

'A thousand years of heritage perished in one night,' Mam continued, conveying the heart-stopping horror of the attack.

Fearing that she would be burned to death, I wanted her to be evacuated to the tranquil Forest of Dean. I thought of Libby's aunt Ada huddling in the church shelter before it was blown to pieces.

'Can't Mam stay with us, Rita?' I implored. 'She won't be any trouble.' They laughed heartily at the declaration before discerning my anxiety. Mam bent down and took my hands, 'I have important work to do back home, sweetheart, helping the war effort.' There was a sense of pride in the way she spoke which lifted my spirits.

'Dad's away fighting in Europe and I do voluntary work, collecting clothing for people who've lost their homes.'

When Annie started singing, '*Keep the home fires burning,*' we cuddled together to listen to the stirring lyrics.

Buoyed up by the idea of being strong, I resolved to help the war effort. Having an antipathy of knitting and wanting to emulate Rita's adventurous spirit, I decided to collect scrap metal in one of her disused prams. Adam became my comrade in arms and together we traversed the Forest of Dean, collecting aluminium pots and pans from prudent neighbours. Like puffed up frigate birds, we swelled with pride delivering our booty to the depot for recycling. Feeling real solidarity with everyone beating the enemy, we returned home fatigued and exhilarated.

As a reward for our endeavours, Rita took us to see the Osiris Players perform "She Stoops to Conquer" in the village hall. I rushed to the front row, to see the mesmerising transformation of seven plain women into eighteenth-century beauties, foppish beaux and thigh-slapping squires. Britain's first all-female professional theatre company led by the indomitable Nancy Hewins bewitched me with their rollicking antics and unbridled gusto.

Starstruck, I watched them load up the horse and dray with scenery and costumes before darting up to Nancy to ask if I could accompany them on their tour. Streaked in greasepaint, she laughed heartily, 'You're too young at the moment, Jeannie, but never give up on your dreams. As Shakespeare said, '"It is not in the stars to hold our destiny but in ourselves."' These inspiring words resonated in my heart as the company rode jubilantly into the distance.

By the time I returned to the hall, Adam was hunched on a damp chair struggling to breathe. Mr Fraser loomed over him with a forced, loathsome smile, prodding his back. Observing Rita chatting with friends, I crept up behind the sly bully and kicked him hard in the shin. He turned like a stormed-up pig and grabbed me viciously by the wrist. I winced in pain before hurling myself into a laudable, theatrical performance to attract attention.

'Help! Help! He's hurting me,' I howled melodramatically, emulating a skilled player stoking up the audience.

Incensed, fearless Rita stormed across the room. 'Let her go, you brute,' she hollered to the delight of the disbanding audience. With exuberant relish, she bashed Fraser over the head with her parasol before stabbing his wobbly belly with its sharp point. Just as Adam stood to see the exposed bully running for the door, Fraser skidded on the proggy mat into the refreshment table, bringing shards of crockery down on his prostrate body. The hearty sound of rip-roaring laughter filled the hall as he slithered like a snake across the floor to make his escape.

Adam's nightmares returned that night inciting him to howl like an animal trapped in pain. When he started sleepwalking, upturning furniture in an effort to escape, Rita got in touch with his parents. On an awakening May morning, as double white Hawthorne blossom covered the Forest of Dean, Adam returned to the war-ravaged city, ending his days as an evacuee.

Jeannie helped lift the hefty scenery into the van before jumping into the passenger seat. Smiling in remembrance of the intrepid Osiris players, she ruminated on the verity of Nancy's parting words, *"It is not in the stars to hold our destiny but in ourselves."*

Randomly chosen as evacuees, I flourished on happy highways whilst Adam experienced unforgettable pain, Jeannie reflected. As the van picked up speed on the open road, she pulled the old purple ribbon from her dog-eared script and tied it in her hair.

Colour

Cheeseman, with bog brush hair spiking from his bulbous head, sits nonchalantly at the front of the detention room playing games on his mobile. He's the teacher who ran into the gym like a Gestapo thug screaming at us to put our hands in the air whilst a skittish police dog sniffed around for drugs. Bet he's got some stashed away under a pile of unmarked books. I start to draw him on the lower tier maths paper lying menacingly on the desk. Dark squiggles transmute into a sly eyed hedgehog parodying my muse.

A fellow detainee laughs flirtatiously before holding up the mustard nails she's painted behind the screen of a book. I grimace in cheeky camaraderie and turn my face to the dirty window overlooking the playing fields. Robo, the PE teacher is twisting and turning through the year 9 football players like Gazza on speed. It reminds me of the time he whizzed down the corridor on my skateboard straight into the short-sighted lad studying his timetable. With the determination of someone in a cup final, Robo flicks his leg into the air and pelts the ball wide of the goalmouth. Everyone cheers, celebrating the misfortune of the down with the kids, buffoon.

At least he's not a heartless teacher like shifty Hancock who put me in detention. He thought it was clever balling me out in front of the whole class for not doing my homework.

'Stop using your dad's disability as an excuse,' he sneered, triggering me to bolt out of the classroom to avoid punching his sanctimonious face. What does that zombie know about caring for someone with scoliosis of the spine? Bet he doesn't have to bath and dress his dad before coming to school in the morning. Hancock wants the sixth form to be for the academic elite, he thinks I'm a waster, a bummer tarnishing the reputation of the school. Homework becomes irrelevant when Dad gets manic. I ratchet into overdrive, watching his every move in case he hurts himself. 'It's just survival, sir,' I want to say, instead of becoming speechless with embarrassment.

The manicurist struts up to Cheeseman to ask if she can go early to pick the bairns up from the childminder. 'No can do,' he screeches like a hysterical parrot.

'Well, I'm going anyway,' she retorts, 'Mam can't afford to pay for another hour.' I admire her audacity as she flounces out, defiantly chalking up a second mindless detention. Cheeseman turns a funny puce colour and I pull out my art folder to dissipate the tension.

'Catch it, check it, change it,' my counsellor told me in a light, vacuous voice – wish I could change my dad's deteriorating health and the toxicity of school.

It works, the vibrancy of Gaudi's work plunges me into a sea of intense colour, where chromatic blues swirl hypnotically with rousing greens. Eagle-eyed, I stare at the emblazoned designs rippling like sculptures in the sunshine. Thousands of small ceramic discs bedeck the beaming Caso

Batllo proclaiming Gaudi's love of colour. In deathly contrast, an oppressive, grey mobile stands dispirited in the schoolyard crying out to be painted. As Cheeseman dismisses me from the detention room, a pearl of a plan incites me to laugh over his droning voice.

The light-yellow dawn seeps through the blackness illuminating our deed.

I hand the hefty tins of paint to the lads, whispering Gaudi's passionate words, '*The clearest manifestation of death is lack of colour.*'

In the stillness of the morning, they nod in approval of the creed as we obliterate the ghastly grey of the mobile. In honour of Gaudi, I break the skin of the ultra-blue paint and snake it like a river over the flamingo pink prefab.

It stands exotic and proud, a vibrant spectacle in a concrete jungle. Overjoyed, I take a photo for my dad to bring some sunshine into his painful life.

By the time I arrive at school, the headmaster has transformed into Inspector Clouseau, madly circling the yard looking for vital clues to identify the miscreants who have defaced the mobile. He turns pallid at the sight of the ravishing colour and barks out bullish orders to repaint it grey.

'Tom, the heel of your shoe's scuffed in pink,' Adie whispers as we join the crowd relishing the commotion. Clouseau's on it, aided and abetted by shifty Hancock.

'Knew you'd be involved in this, Wilson, not enough to do at home, helping your dad?' he goads. I keep control and mirror his supercilious smile before confessing my part in the thrilling escapade. Like the walking dead, Hancock is totally oblivious to the striking appeal of the mobile. Only when the headmaster announces my suspension does he show delayed elation.

Working from home suits me, I bath and dress Dad as per usual then start painting in the conservatory amidst the pile of rubbish accumulated since Mam's death. Nothing gets thrown away in our time-warped house because everything is tinged with her memory.

I work tirelessly in the soothing chaos, caking the canvasses with discordant colours which harmonise in emerging patterns. Saved from the monotony of school, painting daily imbues me with a galvanising sense of purpose. As I wield the brush in bold rhythmic strokes, *"What I do is me: for that I came,"* resonates in my head, stoking the flame of my ambition.

I look in dismay at the skeletal shell of the Mackintosh Building, the disembowelled jewel of the Glasgow School of Art and imagine it pulsating with life. Animated, eloquent students throng the pavements filling me with awe and dread. Charged by their energy, I steel myself to demonstrate my "passion to the panel", knowing my lack of exhibition visits will disadvantage me in a world of accessible travel. Scotland's the furthest I've been away from home due to impecunity and Dad's illness. He doesn't know about the interview, *one step at a time*, I tell myself, shielding him from debilitating panic.

As I push open the embossed door, I sense Mam willing me forward. *Come on, beautiful boy,* I hear her say, *you can do this.* The dryness in my mouth disjoints my words making me awkward before the assured panel. In professional harmony, they scrutinise my paintings, eulogising the

35

patterned vitality of colour. Knowing they speak my language, with uncharacteristic fluency, I unleash the passion within me.

'Who are your favourite artists, Thomas?' asks an owl-faced woman with purple hair.

'Picasso, Dali, Miro,' I reel off in one strong breath.

'Have you been to Spain to see their work?' she enquires, inviting me to rhapsodise about the brilliance of Mediterranean art galleries. Time elongates and in a low, emotionless voice, I deliver my rehearsed answer to the attentive panel. Only the last question renders me speechless.

'What are your career aspirations, Tom?' asks a genial man trying to lighten the mood. Images of my struggling dad disorientate me before a simple truth hits home.

'To be an ever-evolving artist who inspires others,' I say with hope in my heart.

Encouraged by my ebullient art teacher I continually check my UCAS application fearing cataclysmic rejection. Miss Ritz shrieks in delight when I announce that I have been accepted at the prestigious Glasgow School of Art, alma mater to world-famous artists. A giddy feeling of exhilaration disassembles quickly into nauseous panic, how will dad cope without me? Too on edge for Hancock's class, I cry in the privacy of the toilets before making my way home.

The sound of the piano stops me in my tracks, Mam's favourite tune, "Smile" is being played with touching fluency. Through the crack in the doorway, I see Aunt Josie sitting bolt upright at the piano staring at the photo of her beloved sister.

She turns, radiating instant warmth and affection. 'Wasn't expecting to see you home so early, Tommy, been suspended again?' Josie teases.

'What brings you here in the middle of the week?' I ask, knowing she is a creature of unbreakable habit.

'I need time out,' she says like a child anticipating the naughty step.

'Working in the hospital's exhausting, I've been running on empty since your mam's death.' This candid confession moves me and noticing Dad sitting contentedly in the garden, I pour out the crushing anguish of my dilemma. Josie ruminates calmly, taking in the enormity of the situation before proffering a brave solution.

'We're a family, Tommy, we pull together. I'm ready for a change, I'll move in and take care of your dad. He'll be mortified if you let this golden opportunity go because of him.'

I collapse into the armchair, trembling with relief. 'The Glasgow School of Art, bet your mam's jigging around up there in glee,' she says, hugging me tightly.

Dad's reaction surprises us both. 'Brilliant news,' he enthuses spinning in his wheelchair like a Paralympian. 'I knew about the interview, Tommy, I heard you talking to Adie on the phone. Can't pretend I wasn't worried, you've been like a guardian angel to me. Your granda was a remarkable pitman painter but he didn't have the opportunity to develop his talent. Seize the day, son, Josie will take care of me.'

Josie washes and dresses Dad on the morning of my departure. I hand him my latest painting, a red kite soaring in a multi-coloured sky over the beautiful River Derwent. With bursting pride, he places it unsteadily on the mantelpiece. 'We'll FaceTime every day,' I promise him, 'you'll have a front-row view of student life.'

'You'll do me and your mam proud, bonny lad,' he rejoices, assured of my success.

As the heavily laden car drives down the homely back street, my big-hearted dad shrinks into the distance. Going past my school, the grey mobile sulks in the shade, imbuing me with a sense of fortuitous escape. I feel like an explorer travelling to an exotic land in search of treasure. Mam looks on through Josie's eyes. 'Glasgow School of Art, here we come,' my aunt cheers, rousing me to whoop in delight.

Stronger Together

Walking past the serenity of the bowling green soothed Annie's restlessness to containable order. Only when she reached the resplendent hydrangea did she shudder like a bird with a broken wing. Momentarily, Annie thought of returning home before resuscitating courage propelled her forward. Resolutely, she scurried up the sloping path to the neglected flower bed near the bench. Rampant goose grass choked the lavender, reminding Annie of her long absence from the park. With care, she pulled the straggly weeds from the flowers struggling to survive.

'My dolly wants to help,' a tiny girl proclaimed, thrusting her prized possession into the newly cleared earth. Annie jolted slightly before smiling in appreciation at the jovial interruption.

'Come along, Fleury, the lady's got work to do, she doesn't want you bothering her.'

Like a wise mystic, the child stared into Annie's eyes, 'Why have you been crying?' she asked kindly. Embarrassed by her daughter's intrusive question, the mother retrieved the lop-sided dolly from the flower bed. Watching them skip down the path, cocooned in pleasure, Annie cheered at the sight of their gaiety.

Back in the house, the loud smack of the cat flap cut through the silence blanketing every room. Annie's feline companion strolled across the rug and leapt gracefully to the window-sill behind her chair. Switching on the laptop, she thought of the incongruity of Billy's disappearance and her loneliness without him. The wedding photograph on the sun stroked wall reminded her of their togetherness.

'I'm praying from the bottom of my heart that you make it back home Billy. I know you're suffering but there's nothing you can't tell me,' Annie said.

Seeking companionship from her music, she searched Spotify for Nat King Cole's "Ultimate Collection". His mellifluous voice pleading, 'Answer me,' compelled her to sing aloud for Billy to hear. When the track finished she called out tenderly, 'Listen to my prayer, darling man.'

Billy wiped his running nose on a disintegrating tissue before kneeling carefully by the dead seal, statuesquely beautiful in the scorching sun. He felt a painful affinity with the lifeless mammal, slabbed out in the soft bed of sand. Tenderly, Billy touched the protruding belly of the mystic creature before lying on his back beside it. The vast Northumberland sky, usually so uplifting, wrapped around him intensifying his solitude. He remembered with cutting precision how the escalating debt began; financing a holiday for his mam ere cancer ravaged her bones, paying for Linda's IVF treatment which didn't work, buying a reliable car to get to work in South Shields. All before the borrowing fire-crackered out of control when he lost his job. Billy trembled at the thought of his impotency; how could he tell Annie about the blood-sucking debt built by his own heedless folly. Succumbing to sleep, he dreamt of a masked man hurling Annie's armchair into a van, full of broken furniture. A tight fist of sorrow pressed hard against Billy's chest as the sea snaked like a serpent over his face.

Far off sounds of screeching and laughter lapped into his consciousness, bulwarking his descent. He stirred to see children gleaming with life run triumphantly onto the beach. Stretching and calling, they ran panther-like along the sands. Only the boy with the flaming orange hair trailed behind to kick the choppy surf. Billy thought of Annie, his golden marigold, determined to garden in the park despite the vicious attack. Kicked and punched by a drug-crazed youth, she had staggered back home, to a place of safety. His heart raced at the thought of Annie forgiving her assailant in the reconciliation meeting. Picturing her digging deep into the soil speckled in her blood disturbed the blackness within him, creating small holes for the light to shine through.

'Hey, mister,' called the boy from the water's edge, 'you alright?'

'Just a bit wet,' Billy said, 'nothing to worry about.' And he waved, pacifying the boy and signalling to Annie that he could hear her prayer speaking to him in the wind.

The cat saw him first and bolted through the house like an agile kitten. Annie looked up to see Billy tentatively opening the gate with uncharacteristic hesitancy. In the dimly lit hallway, she hugged his damp body, giving silent thanks for his safe return. Knowing that space and respect had kept their relationship together, Annie did not badger him with questions, instead, she poured Billy a tot of whisky and waited for him to speak.

'We're in a mess lass,' he said plaintively, looking directly into her steadfast eyes. Annie listened carefully, not just with her ears but with her whole being.

'Nothing we can't overcome, bonny lad,' she consoled. 'It's a lot of money £40,000 and I'm not going to say it isn't but we'll seek help and get ourselves sorted. You're home and that's all that matters.'

'I've let you down badly,' he spluttered, relaying intense feelings of guilt.

'No one's perfect, Billy Jackson, you're a good man and I'm lucky to have you.'

'Do you still think that, Annie, after all I've put you through?'

'I do, with all my heart. We're stronger together.' In humble gratitude, he squeezed her hand to show the depth of his love.

'Aye, you're right there,' he reaffirmed, 'we're stronger together.'

His daughter was in the kitchen cooking breakfast when Billy came downstairs. Seeing his slippers made her gasp in delight until she looked up and saw his wan, worn-out face.

'Bloody hell, Dad, you look awful,' she blurted out, unable to contain her distress at seeing him so changed. Hugging him tightly, Linda flinched at the frailness of his body beneath his fresh shirt.

'Lovely to see you hinny,' he professed not wanting to break free. Annie took over at the stove, gladdened to see the heart-warming reunion she feared might never happen. *Billy's no prodigal returning home after reckless living,* she thought, *he's a solid family man, struggling to do his best.*

Bright pink anemones in a glass vase added cheeriness to the breakfast. Without warning, a rush of nausea spoilt Linda's appetite. 'Do you want my sausages, Dad? I don't feel like them today.'

'That's a first,' he joked, avoiding the obvious question he knew would cause her pain.

'I'm going to have a baby,' she said quietly as if in disbelief. No one moved, the mystical timing of the longed-for pregnancy held them entranced. Embracing Linda protectively, Billy felt a fresh wave of shame for abandoning his family, his one source of joy.

Annie spoke excitedly, 'Linda's got something else to tell you, Billy, the tide's turning for the Jacksons.'

'Blaydon Cabs need a new driver, Dad. With the money we saved for IVF, you could buy a taxi.'

Sick with indecision, Billy stumbled, 'I can't take your money pet, you'll need it for the baby.'

'Linda wants you to have the money. With help from a debt counsellor and a job, you'll be back in control, paying your way. Take your chances Billy and fight back.'

'You know all about fighting back lass,' he reflected, drawing strength from her love.

Annie tore the stiff cardboard from the parcel ready to see the gift sent by her attacker. With deliberate calm, she scrutinised the painting; large clusters of creamy-white blossoms covered the canvas.

'It's the hydrangeas in the park, the lad's way of making amends,' she said.

'What will you do with it?' Billy asked, looking at her intently.

'When you've decorated the spare bedroom, I'll hang it up in there, it's too lovely to put away.'

Her words resonated deeply with Billy, 'Thought I might paint a mural for the bairn,' he said. 'A mottled grey seal flapping playfully in a crystal sea.'

'That's the true Jackson spirit.'

'Thanks hinny,' Billy said emotionally. 'I nearly lost everything but your light guided me home.'

Turbulence of Youth

I stood by my sister, watching my niece unpack her belongings in a bare, misshapen room. Toying with time, Leah sluggishly crammed a jumble of clothes in the narrow cupboard adjoining the bathroom. In an effort to personalise the eerie blankness of the space, she placed treasured memorabilia on the shelves.

Persusing a photo of her parents huddled under a tree, "Who will you watch tele with when I'm at uni?" she asked her mother.

'The dog,' my sister stated, exposing the reality of her impending loneliness. Leah overcame the temptation to collapse like a wounded animal onto the bed and continued unpacking with forced vigour.

'I'll call you every day,' she said warmly.

Overlapping voices in the corridor heralded the dreaded call. 'All freshers to the quad,' rang as a death knell, making my sister gasp before immense pride grounded her. She watched in silence as Leah, a tiny figure in-the-midst of gangly boys, walked outside to begin life away from home.

In fading autumnal light, my sister hastened to the car trying to hide her fragility.

45

'I'll miss her,' she confided, 'Leah's been my world since Jack died.'

'You'll be together in spirit and share the joy of her journey. Leah will carry on enriching your life in so many ways.'

'I know,' my sister conceded, 'but it's still hard.'

Distracting hunger turned our minds to the pub, home to British bonhomie and delectable beer. We chose a table close to the bustling bar, wanting to be immersed in frivolity to dissipate our sadness. 'You were such a child when you started uni,' my sister reminisced.

'Oh, but it was exciting,' I said, recalling the thrill of leaving home to explore a groovy, mercurial city. In my heart, I felt like a mighty pioneer, desperate for new land and rollicking adventure. 'It was a lot of fun you know, Liverpool in the 70s when punk rock got going. One minute I was a sweet girl with a pigtail and a quilted dressing gown that zipped right up to my neck and the next, I was a high booted, pogo dancing queen. Great anarchic exuberance – just what you need in your youth.'

'You were lucky, I got to stay at home with Mum and Dad, riding my moped to the old people's home was the height of my rebellion.'

'You had a good time in your own way. There's only so much jumping up and down you can do before life plants your feet firmly on the ground.'

'Strange how you just came home that night, walked into the kitchen as if you'd never been away.'

'Events,' I sighed, comprehending the fortuity of my return.

I thought of my younger, unformed self, mutating freely in the vibrancy of punk power with its feisty fearlessness and rampant energy. 'It worries me that the kids are so conformist these days, they've been brainwashed by dullards into being work automatons. I hope Leah becomes an untamed free spirit at uni.'

'Wish I'd had the chance to be irresponsible and fun-loving. When you were parading around like a demented panda with bog brush hair, I was dispensing tablets to the hamsters in the nursing home.'

'That was the best bit, the transformation. I loved cobbling an outfit together, teaming up a ripped T-shirt with a sassy skirt.'

'Dressing to please yourself, far cry from my doll-like uniform.'

'You were a great nurse and I was a punk warrior, a headstrong, pogoing phenomenon.'

'Sounds amazing, can't think why you came back to sleepy old Worcester.'

'Overnight, I metamorphosed into a new self and simply fluttered home.'

On the train, the light clacking of the wheels on the track lulled me into a ruminative state of mind.

Character is destiny, repeated like a prophetic mantra in my head as I saw Leah's smiling face in the grubbiness of the window. With sure-footed agility, she would vault the turbulence of youth and land unscathed on solid ground. I thought of my own heady journey and miraculous escape from lurking danger. *What forces throw us back on course*, I wondered, *when we stumble headlong into darkness.*

Thanks to "the Fab Four" and rampant Beatlemania, Liverpool had an intoxicating familiarity which quashed my sense of arrival. Seeing Strawberry Field and lively Penny Lane felt like being reunited with treasured friends. Released from the constraints of home, I revelled in the halcyon days of youthful discovery. In modish pubs, rapid banter unfettered my small-town voice, imbuing me with gutsy confidence. Full of punk powered energy, I pogoed in tribal synchronicity to stormy lyrics fomenting a sea of change. Wild fun engulfed me in blind invincibility before sharks gathered in the water.

Getting ready that night seemed like any other, except for a tight feeling of anticipation. I tousled my hair in the sassy style of Debbie Harry before applying gleaming blue eyeshadow.

Trudy smiled at herself in the mirror, liking the look of the oversized jacket which swamped her gaudy orange dress. "Atomic" by Blondie, played seductively in the background whilst I strutted around in glamorous high heels before retrieving a mini skirt from the discarded pile of clothes on the floor. Going to the Hacienda in Manchester was a big deal and we wanted edgy, sultry outfits for the magnificence of the evening we envisaged.

By the time we stood on the East Lancs Road ready to hitchhike, we had metamorphosed into exotic creatures of the night. The lads who picked us up looked like distorted puppets with ugly teeth and wonky smiles. As the driver manically increased his speed around a dangerous bend, I clutched the dirty fabric of the seat. Trudy, enjoying the thrill of the ride began talking in a quick, flirtatious way to the weirdo who kept leering at her in his mirror. Stepping into the sharp coolness of the air, I noticed her handing him a scrap of paper which he scrutinised with his small, piggy eyes.

Other memories of that insane escapade unravel like a distorted film strip. I remember smoking a bubbling hooker pipe in a gloomy room before bolting at breakneck speed down a darkened alley. Shrieking with laughter, we hobbled like conjoined twins over the gravelly stones spiking our feet.

The palatial Hacienda was the mecca of all dance clubs, the promised land of joyous revelling. Exciting, new sounds lashed around the steel columns in the transformed warehouse charging us with frantic energy. With unabandoned delight, we danced fervently under the bright lights of innocence.

I was seated at a book laden table studying Edward Albee when Trudy rang the doorbell. Standing defensively, with bloody, self-bitten lips, she talked in a staccato manner about the driver we met whilst hitchhiking. I listened in hazy disbelief as Trudy recounted how the night before, down by the river, he had pushed her into thorny grass and like a beast, raped her.

'I'm not going to report it to the police,' she said emphatically.

'In court, it would look as if I was complicit. I gave him my address and went willingly with him to a remote place. It was madness not seeing the danger.'

'You didn't deserve to be raped, Trudy, report the brute.'

'And be gaslit, like I'm the one on trial?' Knowing our fun-loving world had been shattered by a blast of reality, as wounded comrades, we held each other tight.

When Trudy crossed the Mersey to plant her feet firmly in Birkenhead, I packed my bags to return home. Braver and wiser than my younger self, I walked through the morning mist shrouding the Liverpool streets, towards my future.

My sister spoke in a broken voice down the telephone, 'She's gone, Cub, flown the nest.'

'It's difficult letting go but Leah's made of tough metal, yours and Jack's. Keep the candle burning and she'll come back stronger,' I assured her, as my past pogoed into the present.

Spring

Danny deliberately left his cagoule in the hallway so the biting November rain could penetrate deep into his body. The lightness of his school bag felt strangely liberating, what did he care if the marked A level essays were still on the kitchen table. In the blanketing darkness of the morning, Danny moved quickly to his car trying to build momentum for the coming day. With trembling hands, he wiped aside the wet hair streaking into his face before reversing recklessly into the lamppost opposite his house. His grip on the steering wheel tightened, creating a vicious tension which stabbed at the back of his eyes. Danny held rigidly still, not bothering to wipe away the tears blearing his vision.

He planned to pull in safely to the side of the road but instead, slammed the car into first gear and headed to the hills.

The children sat pixie-like on their little cushions, eager for their teacher to finish the magical story started before break. Big, wondrous eyes stared up at Lucy as she ceremoniously lifted the book from the cupboard and placed it on her desk. A blissful silence permeated the room before her melodious voice spoke the first mystical words: 'Summer slumbered peacefully as autumnal winds whipped russet red leaves from the tree. Rose clung bravely to a thorny stem, watching her petals twirl in the crispy cold air.' Tiny fingers fell uniformly from mouths to nestle in laps as the story continued. 'A cooing wood pigeon brushed past her, desperate to escape the hissing cat hunched in the grass.' Lucy thought about Danny's suicide and imagined him swooping through the sky screeching for help. Only the children's awe and wonder brought her back to the schoolroom.

'When darkness settled on her fallen petals, Rose dropped her shrunken head and fell asleep,' she whispered.

By lunchtime, Lucy was losing her composure so instead of eating, she pinned the children's paintings on the wall. Julie called from the corridor, 'Give yourself a break and come up to the staff room.' Lucy trembled at the thought of being in such an intimate, exposing space.

'I'd love to,' she said convincingly, 'but Ruth wants new displays up by the end of the week. No rest for the wicked.' Lucy's utterance accentuated raw feelings of guilt relating to Danny's suicide. She lamented the sickening obsession with work which had effaced all signs of his suffering. In her brother's darkest hour, she had failed to see the pain which led him to the brooding hills. Swirls of colour from the paintings rotated in her mind to form the cavernous quarry which swallowed up Danny's body.

Lucy could see the children chasing around outside, merry in the brightness of the rippling sunshine. Telling Ryan she didn't want children hadn't been easy. Usually warm and gregarious, he had frozen in fear as if perusing a stranger. Her own lacerating words echoed back to her, *I'm not, not fit, to be a mother.* Lucy affirmed her unworthiness to bring a child into the world when she had not been there to ease the pain of her beloved brother.

Ryan's leaving was a fitting retribution after her cruel rebuff and ongoing, erratic rage.

She experienced a different sort of bereavement without him as if her body had been cracked open to ooze loneliness. The shrillness of the whistle cut across her rumination, startling her back into action. Dutifully, she placed the pictures on the children's desks and waited expectantly for their return.

'Miss, I don't like the snake looking so sad,' Anna said in a doleful voice. Lucy felt afresh the potency of the story, *"Heartbroken by the wintry stillness of Rose, Snake buried his head under a moist heap of decaying leaves."*

'Look how joyful he is in this picture,' she instructed, 'Snake's brimming with happiness when Rose unfurls her velvety red petals in glorious spring.' Anna's bright blue eyes blazed with wonder, quelling Lucy's lurching despair. She knelt down at the table nearest to her wanting to savour the children's delight.

'Look, Miss, I've given my snake a red head so he looks like a rosebud,' Tony enthused.

'Such a wonderful idea,' she replied, marvelling at the boy's ingenuity.

'My snake's eating the rose because he's hungry,' boasted Liam, trying to puff out his skinny chest.

'Poor Rose!' Lucy exclaimed. 'They're in love, Liam, which means they're tender to one another.' Unable to comprehend the sweetness of love, the boy laughed at the silliness of her comment.

Lucy saw herself as a ravenous snake eating away at the sanctity of her marriage. Learning about Danny's gambling addiction had blanketed her in shame. She had not known about the crucifying debt which robbed him of dignity until she read the heart-wrenching suicide note left in his car. On the point of collapse, Lucy gripped the back of a tiny chair as a strong beam of yellow light streaked into the classroom. Still and silent, in-the-midst of the children, she felt the radiating strength of her brother's love.

'Miss, do you like mine?' Alison questioned, pointing to the colourful splodges on her paper. 'I'm gonna give it to me dad,' she continued, stirring Lucy to think of Ryan.

With dragonfly agility, she swept through the children to search for her mobile phone buried deep in her bag. Pacifying the class with effusive praise and a bright smiley face, Lucy speedily typed;

"So sorry, yearning to see you again xxx."

She looked intently at the children's drawings of the budding rose returning to the snake after the long winter months and felt the quiet thrill of her own burgeoning spring.

The old black rainbow lodged in Lucy's brain filled with colour as she journeyed home.

At the sight of Ryan's car in the driveway, a weird mixture of relief and apprehension made her heart race. As she entered the house, the upbeat reggae blaring from the kitchen gave her hope of reconciliation.

Industriously preparing the evening meal, Ryan was oblivious to Lucy's presence until she touched him on the shoulder. Slowing down time, he turned off the music before facing her with purply bruised eyes. The space between them solidified into a menacing presence. 'I'm sorry,' Lucy said, trying to soften the pain she had inflicted on him.

'You were hurting, I should have supported you better.'

'I felt so guilty about Danny's death, all that suffering I didn't notice.'

'You were buried in schoolwork, blocking everything out, including me.'

'How did I manage to go so wrong?'

'It's the job, you let it take too much out of you. We'd lost our way long before Danny's suicide and when the bad times came, we had nothing left in reserve.'

The truth of his words roused Lucy from wintry slumber. 'When you said you didn't want children, I felt like you were riding rough shod over my emotions. Men have feelings too you know.'

'Does this mean you're not coming back?'

'If you let me in, I'll be there for you but I can't be a stranger in my own home.'

A line from Ryan's favourite poem crackled through Lucy's icy thoughts. '*Ah, love, let us be true. To one another!*'[4] she said with a sudden burst of energy.

Her heartfelt plea filled Ryan with joy. After the long darkness of winter, his radiant rose was unfurling anew.

---

[4] From *Dover Beach* by Matthew Arnold. First published 1867, although some sources point to 1849.

All in Gold

Hearing the unexpected news, Jude felt crushing, childlike sorrow. 'See you on holiday, Grandma,' Rosie called out on Skype, unaware of the constraining nature of chickenpox. *A cruel twist of fate*, Jude thought fighting back the tears; France without the bairn's sunshine seemed unimaginable after weeks of mounting excitement.

Despite the setback, holiday spirits were high as the diminished family party drove around the streets of Fayence searching for "Villa Harmonie". Scrutinising the online photographs whilst her husband drove along steep, narrow roads, Jude failed to recognise the house awaiting their arrival. Only on the descent from the village was she able to identify the coral building with smiling mint shutters as their chosen abode.

The caretaker, shuffling around in well-worn moccasins spoke of the house with profound love as if it was a treasured friend. Leisurely imparting useful information to enrich their stay, he ushered them through the chic bedrooms with rustic high beamed ceilings. Jude admired the forest green pine trees opening out like gigantic umbrellas on the horizon and felt a glow of pride in finding such a special place for the family to enjoy. Downstairs, a soft blue light bathed the back of the house evoking a soulful serenity omitted from the photographs. As the gate shutters closed on the caretaker's tooting car, the family cheered in expectant delight.

In relaxed holiday mood, Jude and her daughter meandered through the backstreets of Fayence, stopping to admire the cats luxuriating in the evening sunshine. Following Fabian's instructions, they reached the top of a gruelling hill to a see a revelrous village bustling with activity. Whilst an aged rock band blasted out Rolling Stones lyrics, models paraded jubilantly in simple homemade clothes.

Nicole beamed at the ragbag fashion show enthralling the locals, 'Dad would have loved this,' she said. Jude pictured him cocooned in the car, patiently returning to the airport to collect his sister.

Hearing "Honky Tonk Women", they sprang into action, rocking like giddy teenagers to the compelling music. When the track ended, a petite lady with a noticeably small head and big doll-like eyes approached them. 'You must be English,' she said, 'I can tell by the way you dance.' They laughed heartily at her astute deduction.

'My name is Marie-Claire and I live in Seillans with my husband who is at home finishing a painting.'

Jude was impressed by her willingness to engage so openly with complete strangers. 'You must come around and visit us,' she offered, producing a business card that stated she was a *Professeur de Langues*. In a fun atmosphere of bonhomie, Marie-Claire kissed them on both cheeks and repeated the invitation.

'Give me a ring before you come and I'll give you directions to my house, it can be difficult to find,' she purred in an exquisite French accent. They stood transfixed as Marie-Claire, wafting mystique, sauntered down the sloping street.

Leaving other family members to trawl the splendours of the Fayence market, Jude and Nicole, plunged into the pool of hospitality to visit their new friend. Seillans, a village nestling at the base of a forested mountain, overlooked rolling plains edged by slender cypress trees. Marie-Claire gesticulated in a uniquely French way to express her pleasure at their arrival.

'Magnifique,' she exclaimed, leading them onto a slightly raised terrace adjacent to the pool. To their delight, an appetising lunch of fish and avocado salad was laid out on a table draped in a bright blue cloth. Captivated by the burst of colour, mother and daughter abandoned their English reserve to savour the joy of the occasion.

'Pierre is in Cannes, delivering his latest painting to a buyer,' Marie-Claire explained, handing round the copper breadbasket.

'The climate and luminescent light make the South of France an artist's paradise. I chose to move here from Paris when my first husband died, I met Pierre at a jazz club in Nice. There he was sitting on the floor, absorbed in the music, just when I was thinking love would never come my way again.'

'I'm sorry to hear about your first husband,' Jude said, wanting to acknowledge Marie-Claire's loss.

'I feel his presence all around me, especially in Fayence which had a special place in Richard's heart. It's where his grandfather was accidentally parachuted to in the war.'

'I know the story,' Nicole reflected, 'Dad mentioned it to me when he was researching the area.'

'Miraculously, allied forces were dropped in the wrong place because of a communication failure. With help from the resistance, they joined the soldiers clearing the Germans from high ground to the north of the village and the crossroads at Quatre Chemins. After intense fighting, helped by a fortuitous twist of fate, Fayence was liberated.'

'And Richard's grandfather was one of those parachutists,' Nicole remarked.

'Yes, it was thanks to him that we first visited this exquisite part of France.'

'It's picture perfect,' Jude said, awed by the array of green woodland crowning the horizon.

'Seillans has become my place of solace,' Marie-Claire confided, fixing her eyes on the lofty, silvery mountains.

Like old friends, they fell into natural silence, contemplating the rolling force of circumstance.

'It was heart-warming to see you dancing so freely to the Rolling Stones music,' Marie-Claire enthused. 'Richard used to sing their songs to me.'

The mystery solved, Marie-Claire didn't see them as strangers, more like *amies spéciales* from the past. 'Richard was a free spirit, he died skiing off-piste in the French Alps. With his guidance, I found this beautiful house in Seillans, only a short distance from where his grandfather landed in the war.' Musical chimes hanging from a parasol stirred evocatively in the wind.

'C'est la vie,' she added nobly, recognising the interwoven fabric of life.

The visit impacted on Jude, Marie-Claire's contentment made her feel more at ease, more carefree. On a whim, she suggested the family delay their trip to Genoa to visit the Chagall museum passionately recommended by her French friend. Wanting a car free day, Nicole and her aunty opted to stay in the tranquil villa.

After a hazardous drive through urban Nice, Cimiez Hill stood like a beacon of calm above the city. In the museum, Jude marvelled at the natural light pouring into the simple, pared-down interiors. Just as Marie-Claire had narrated, bold dreamscapes of immense power graced the walls.

'Stirring paintings. No print can do Chagall's work justice,' Neil said. They perused the intertwined lovers lying on the back of Pegasus, holding flowers in outstretched hooves like a splendid bride.

'Chagall a prophet of love,' Neil lauded, placing an arm around Jude's waist.

'I didn't know his first wife died suddenly,' she said, thinking of Marie-Claire's unforeseen loss.

'Bella has flown over my pictures for many years guiding my art,' Neil read aloud, conjuring up her presence in the room. Jude surveyed the vast canvasses, 'Such energy blazing from Chagall's dazzling use of colour,' she observed. 'A divine message of hope.'

In the peaceful garden, Neil sat in the sunshine admiring the shiny, green olive trees twisting on the lawn. He ignored his ringing phone as he watched Jude smelling the fringed lavender bordering the grass. By the time she reached the table, he was reading the shocking message left by Nicole: 'Horrific news, the Morandi bridge in Genoa collapsed at 11:30 this morning. Thank God we changed our plans, we could have been there!' In stunned silence, they read details of the tragedy on Neil's phone.

A section of the Morandi bridge has fallen 45 metres, along with dozens of vehicles amid heavy traffic.

Harrowing images of strewn cars in mangled rubble recorded the terrifying scale of the tragedy. Rescue workers searching for the living and the dead, appeared dwarfed by huge boulders of broken bridge. A sepia photo of the viaduct in the mist with a huge chunk missing seemed eerily apocalyptic.

'Oh, Neil, what a wretched disaster,' Jude cried, 'those poor people.'

'We've had a miraculous escape!' he exclaimed, visibly shaken.

Jude visualised Marie-Claire dressed all in gold, blessing her with good fortune in the charmed streets of Fayence. 'I'm glad I dance like an English woman,' she said, clasping Neil with ardent love.

A Candle in The Dark

As I reached for the remote hidden beneath a plethora of newspaper supplements, a young Syrian orphan spoke directly to the camera. 'People don't like refugees here; they throw stones and call us names. I want to go somewhere I will feel safe and welcome.' The tragedy of the boy's plight stirred potent memories of the Kindertransport which rescued me from genocide.

'We will come for you, Elias, as soon as we can,' my mother cried out, as the train pulled away. The words clung to me like a lifesaving oxygen mask. I saw my father catch her falling body before they disappeared out of sight. Hiding my tears, I fixated on the label attached to my coat declaring my name and number. The playing of a flute reminded me of the Pied Piper of Hamelin who lured the children to the top of the mountain where they disappeared forever. Icy cold fear gripped me, nulling my hunger. I thought of the special packed lunch buried in my bag and longed for the serenity of home before the smashing of the glass. It was difficult to understand why my parents hadn't come with me to escape the violence and name-calling. Like other children clasping talismans of comfort, I held my father's watch in my hand as it marked the slow passage of time. I was not the brave boy he wanted me to be, the formal rigidity of the soldiers was unsettling. A feeling of abandonment rattled through the carriage as the train sped further away from home.

When we got to Holland, some of the children cheered excitedly because we'd escaped the Nazis. 'Do you know what this means, Elias?' demanded a spirited girl, underestimating my ability to comprehend the significance of our journey.

'Yes,' I replied stoically. 'We are the children of the Kindertransport, on our way to a new life in England free from persecution.' These were the words uttered by my parents as they conjured up the strength to let me go and I said them freely as children do when they emulate adults.

Imagined terrors haunted my young mind; I felt sure that our heavily laden boat would sink without trace into the dark depths of the ocean. Placing my feet firmly on English soil came as a blessed relief until I saw a double-decker bus moving unsteadily down a crowded street. Deathly blood-red, I imagined it toppling over and crushing me to the ground. Only when I saw an older boy crying unashamedly did I determine to be strong.

On the television, the Syrian boy looked like a fretful old man, worried about the future. 'Children are being stranded at refugee centres, unable to seek asylum or reach their families who live in the UK,' the broadcaster said.

Why are there scarce safe and legal routes for innocents to escape the horror of war? I questioned. *10,000 children were welcomed into Britain as part of the Kindertransport operation, prior to the outbreak of the Second World War.*

I was lucky being sent to live with Bill and Nell in glorious Worcestershire. Despite my crippling anxiety, their kindness eased me to a place of acceptance and growth. Restless at first, I returned repeatedly to the train station desperate for my mother to keep her promise. But she didn't step from the carriage to wrap her loving arms around me, instead, she stayed incarcerated in Germany like an animal awaiting slaughter.

After a painful transitional period, when the letters stopped arriving, I let go in order to survive.

Fruit picking with Nell was life-enhancing. As the deep purple currants fell rapidly into shiny white paper, she sang her favourite song, '*One of these mornings you're gonna rise up singing, and you'll spread your wings and take to the sky.*' In the fields, in harmony with nature, Nell taught me to relish the awakening moments of true happiness. At lunchtime, we perched like hungry birds in our straw nests devouring thick slabs of bread with corned beef and sweet-tasting tomatoes. She unscrewed the top of the Tizer bottle as if uncorking Sekt and enjoying the sense of communion the ritual brought, I waited patiently for my turn to drink the fizzy nectar.

Bill was a talented gardener and I remember how skilfully he trailed yellow roses that shone like muted stars over a wooden arch. But the cricket was best of all. In immaculate grounds, we listened to the hypnotic thwack of leather against the hardness of the bat, united in our love of the beautiful game.

Even when I learnt that my parents had died in the Bergen-Belsen concentration camp along with 50,000 other people, I just got on with life. I had lived with my loss since the outbreak of the war when their communication ceased.

Only at Bill's funeral service when the priest delivered the eulogy did I begin to think about the life they didn't live.

'To everything, there is a season, and a time to every purpose under heaven: A time to be born, a time to die.' Memories of my father's vitality shattered my composure. I saw his radiant smile as I wobbled unsteadily towards him on my Christmas bicycle. In the prime of his life, when "Germany for the Germans" became a hate-filled doctrine, he was exterminated for being Jewish.

A much-loved doctor in Leipzig, a saver of lives, he was wiped from this Earth in the darkest of times and I was oblivious to his passing.

'A time to mourn,' rang out like a clamorous bell calling me to confront my past.

Remembering the relief I felt when my parents didn't come for me filled me with immense guilt. My close friend Klaus hid in the smelly confines of the outdoor toilet as his mother wailed out his name. 'I don't want to go to America,' he bellowed in rage, trying to avert his fate. As they bundled him into the waiting car, he lashed out like a captured animal before waving resignedly to his foster parents. Nell embraced her bereft friends in her thick arms, stoically soaking up their pain. Buoyed up by my good fortune, I deliberately blocked out memories of my own family and settled heartily into English village life.

"Happy as the grass was green"[5], I pounded up the hills before rolling down like a dislodged haystack to the river

---

[5] From *Fern Hill* by Dylan Thomas. Orignally published in Horizon Magazine in 1945. First appeared in book form in *Deaths and Entrances* (Joseph Malaby Dent, 1945)

where, in boyhood wonder, I gazed at the cast-iron bridge on the horizon.

When I graduated with a first-class degree in engineering, Bill and Nell stood proudly by my side for the milestone photograph that recorded my triumph. Intent on moving forward, I buried my German past, wanting the dark shadows to fall behind me. Even with the birth of my son, who looked remarkably like my father, I refused to acknowledge my German roots in case a permeating sadness sapped my strength. Bereavement though, heightens emotions and as the priest eulogised Bill for his generosity and warmth, in the cool confines of the church, I thought of the divine uniqueness of my own father. My dear "vater" whose photograph lay buried, forgotten in the attic.

Lifting the lid from the stained box was physically painful as aspects of my own self collided, reducing me in size. Only when I saw the photograph of my father holding me up to the heavens like a prize trophy did I breathe in new life. Seeing the radiating beauty of my mother after crippling years of denial, I felt blessed to be the child of such remarkable parents. My son, with wisdom beyond his years, didn't ask why I'd hidden such treasures away, instead, he perused the photographs with venerable concentration.

'I look like Grandad,' he said, feeling an immediate connection with the young German man pulsating with life. As we talked freely about my parents, I understood what a huge sacrifice they had made putting their only son on the train to freedom. Thanks to their valour and the incredible kindness of the British people, I was saved from the Holocaust.

I heard Benesh say that she had been in makeshift accommodation for three years, since her parents were killed by the Taliban. 'Now we have left the EU, there are no safe and legal routes for child refugees without families here to reach Britain,' the reporter said. 'Some of the children are sleeping rough in the snow, in derelict buildings and in overcrowded tents. Others have risked their lives to make it to these shores. One boy made it to the UK by clinging to the wheel arch of a coach, centimetres from the engine. Another came in a freezer and spent the whole journey thinking he would die.'[6] *Where's the spirit of compassion that blazed so strongly in the Second World War,* I wondered, *when did loving hearts turn to stone?*

'Don't turn your back on these children,' I implored the squirming politician on the screen. 'Give them a place of shelter, hope and love.' In the sanctuary of my English home, Bill's saying came forcibly to mind, *"A candle loses none of its light by lighting another."*

---

[6] *Revealed: 10,000 child refugees risked their lives to enter Britain.* Published in The Guradian, 11 Jan, 2020

Wind Horse

Maggie smiled to think that Frank was out on the beach enjoying the last rays of summer. With the sun warming her face, she watched the unfettered children bound past him into the sea. It delighted her that Frank's white cremation urn looked like a giant ice cream in the sand. To her amusement, a barrel-chested seagull circled around it with sharp, quizzical eyes.

Maggie took the urn to the water's edge so the rippling waves could wash over it. 'When the family come home, we'll scatter your ashes in a special place,' she whispered to Frank. Ever so slowly, as if time had no consequence, Maggie dried the urn with the edge of her skirt. 'Let's go home now,' she said, half expecting Frank to pick up her basket and carry it to the car.

Alone in the garden, Maggie snatched zealously at the eerie goose grass clinging to the soil. Long, hairy branches trailed spider-like from her arms before she threw them dismissively onto the compost heap. Reaching for her water, Maggie saw the beauty of Frank's work; tall bearded irises brushing against the sundial, red velvety gillyflowers clustered by the stone wall. Everything carefully planned to create an oasis of wonder. She thought forlornly about the house viewings and the trail of strangers traipsing into their sanctuary.

'Oh, Frank,' Maggie cried, 'I don't want a new beginning in some strange place.' Immediate feelings of guilt ensnared her; it was selfish to think of her own needs when downsizing meant she could give Lauren the deposit for a house. The baby was crawling in a cramped, soulless flat whilst she sat alone in capacious rooms.

Breathing deeply, Maggie tried to circumvent the pain she was feeling whilst packing Frank's holiday shirts into a charity bag. Holding a carrot-orange one, she was reminded of his exuberance and joy.

Maggie heard Frank's jocular voice regaling his favourite tale of being in the bunker as a German soldier pounded the soil above. She knew that his experiences in the war had imbued him with a steadfast appreciation for the sanctity of life. Unable to part with the evocative shirt, Maggie placed it lovingly on the floor. The dog, excited by her obvious change in mood, tossed his raggy monkey playfully into her lap. Throwing it instinctively into the air, she was arrested by the brilliant force of the cherry blossom flowering in rich profusion. A feeling of belonging wrapped protectively around her as if cocooning her from an impending storm.

Pleased to be standing in her familiar place in the choir, Maggie drew strength from being part of a relaxed, purposeful group. Laughter gave way to immediate concentration as the conductor magicked an ethereal sound of purity into the cavernous space. She listened intently, working hard to master the technique before singing powerfully to propel herself forward. Feeling a deep connection with the rousing words, Maggie skilfully threaded her vocals into the choral tapestry. '*Praise to the holiest in the height and in the depth be praise,*' she sang defiantly to break through the darkness of her grief.

Communing open-heartedly with the congregation, Maggie appreciated being a small part of something bigger than herself. The music swelled to magnificence as the choir proclaimed, '*In all his words most wonderful; most sure in all his ways.*' Seeing the loving pride in her daughter's eyes, she felt like an adulated child revelling in applause. With tender gratitude, Maggie received the soft kiss Lauren blew before exiting cautiously through the hefty doors.

Alone in the house, a hounding melancholy stirred menacingly with the joy of the evening. Preoccupied, Maggie involuntarily placed two mugs side by side to make the supper drinks. Returning Frank's to the cupboard she started to emit a strange wailing sound which echoed around the kitchen. Reoccurring thoughts of leaving their cherished home made her tremble in fear. It would be like a second, insufferable bereavement. Memories of Lauren's loving visit intensified feelings of mauling selfishness. Tight, painful tears blurred Maggie's vision as two titanic aspects of her own desires collided, making it difficult for her to breathe. Fortuitously, the dog's incessant barking jerked her back into action.

Entering the living room to pacify him, she saw Frank's smiling face in the prominently placed photograph, radiating warmth and understanding. Maggie smiled back, embarrassed by her bout of insanity after such a triumphant evening. Stroking the dog, she thought of Frank's story about riding the Wind Horse through the turbulence of life with stability and calm. *Take it easy hinny,* Maggie heard him say.

Imagine a horse galloping through a beautiful meadow, feel that life force running through you. Be courageous and strong.

With all her might, she harnessed her powerful emotions and imagined cantering on to rich, new pastures.

Much to Maggie's relief, the phone rang earlier than she'd expected. Hearing Lauren's cheerful voice was restorative. She was delighted to hear that Alice was sleeping better now she was scuttling around the flat like a little crab.

'Mum, thanks so much for my lovely stay, sorry I had to leave the concert early to catch the train. I thought the singing was amazing by the way, I'm so proud of you.' Maggie was touched by the effusive praise before the ensuing question stunned her into silence.

'You seem so at home in the choir, are you sure you want to move?'

Maggie pinned her eyes on the pink blossom hanging from the tree and breathed deeply. In the pivotal moment, she felt the life force of the Wind Horse running through her. 'Oh, darling, I hope you're not too disappointed but I don't want to leave the North East just yet. I'm sorry to change my mind but I feel this is where I belong.'

'Well, good for you, being so honest with yourself. I was surprised you thought about moving in the first place when you've got so many friends up there.'

'It's just that I hoped to downsize and give you some money for a deposit on a house,' Maggie finally disclosed. 'Maybe I could release some equity instead.'

'Mum, that's not your worry,' Lauren replied emphatically.

'Anyway, we've decided we don't want to buy a featureless box in London. Plus, we're not sure it's the right place to bring up Alice, it's so polluted and congested. We really miss the countryside and the coast, maybe we should take the plunge and move back home.'

'But what about your jobs?' Maggie asked earnestly.

'Joe can relocate easily with the Environment Agency and yes, it will be harder for me but I'm sure I can find work now I've built up my CV. It's just an idea, but if we did get jobs in Newcastle, do you think we could stay with you until we've saved for a deposit on a house?'

Maggie felt elated knowing the Wind Horse had weathered the storm and was riding on to fresh, green meadows. 'I can't think of anything I'd like more,' she said, looking at Frank's uplifting photograph.

'Thanks, Mum, Alice will love it. I'll talk it over with Joe but I know he'll be thrilled.'

After a slight pause, and an obvious change of voice to ameliorate the pain, Lauren asked calmly, 'Have you thought any more about where you want to scatter Dad's ashes?'

Maggie stroked the feather white urn, 'I've decided out on the moors in Blanchland.' She pictured spreading Frank's ashes over rampant purple heather beneath a vast Northumberland sky. A resting place of tranquil beauty far from the beaches of Dunkirk for her noble soulmate. 'When you come home, we'll climb to the top where the heavens meet the land,' Maggie said, 'and scatter the ashes together.'